FREDDIE MOLE ★ LION TAMER

FREDDIE MOLE
LION TAMER

ALEXANDER McCALL SMITH

Illustrated by Kate Hindley

Delacorte Press

Text copyright © 2016 by Alexander McCall Smith
Jacket art copyright and interior illustrations © 2016 by Kate Hindley

All rights reserved. Published in the United States by Delacorte Press, an imprint of Random House Children's Books, a division of Penguin Random House LLC, New York. Originally published in paperback in the UK by Bloomsbury Publishing Plc, London, in 2016.

Delacorte Press is a registered trademark and the colophon is a trademark of Penguin Random House LLC.

Visit us on the Web! rhcbooks.com

Educators and librarians, for a variety of teaching tools, visit us at RHTeachersLibrarians.com

Library of Congress Cataloging-in-Publication Data
Names: McCall Smith, Alexander, author. | Hindley, Kate, illustrator.
Title: Freddie Mole, lion tamer / Alexander McCall Smith ; illustrated by Kate Hindley.
Other titles: Lion tamer
Description: First American edition. | New York : Delacorte Press, [2018] | Summary: When Freddie gets a job at the circus to help his family financially, he is surprised—and frightened—to learn he will be the understudy for some of the acts.
Identifiers: LCCN 2017027309 (print) | LCCN 2017039693 (ebook) | ISBN 978-1-5247-1379-9 (ebook) | ISBN 978-1-5247-1377-5 (trade hardcover)
Subjects: | CYAC: Circus—Fiction. | Courage—Fiction. | Family life—Fiction.
Classification: LCC PZ7.M47833755 (ebook) | LCC PZ7.M47833755 Fre 2018 (print) | DDC [Fic]—dc23

The text of this book is set in 13-point Candida.
Interior design by Trish Parcell

Printed in the United States of America
10 9 8 7 6 5 4 3 2
First American Edition

This book is for George Lockhart.

* ★ ★ ★

This is a picture of a boy called Freddie Mole. He lived quite a few years ago. At the time of this story, he was about ten— or maybe a bit younger or even a bit older. That doesn't matter too much. The important thing was that Freddie Mole was a kind boy who everybody liked.

Nobody had a bad word to say about him, and there were plenty of people who were happy to call him their friend.

Freddie lived with his father, Ted Mole, and with his twin brother and sister, Ned and Bella, who were much younger than Freddie. He helped his father and his grand-mother look after the twins because their mother, Flora Mole, had gone off to sea to earn money for the family. She was one of those people who work on great ocean lin-ers, making up the bunks and cleaning the cabins of the passengers. She wore a white uniform for this, and she worked very hard. She was often away for month after month—sometimes for as long as a year. When she came back she was always very tired from all her hard work and would sleep for a whole day and a whole night before her strength returned. Only then was she able to smile again. "Oh, my darlings," she would say, "it's so good to be home."

"Where is Ma today?" Freddie sometimes asked his father, and Ted would point to the map of the world he kept on the kitchen wall. This would have a pin in it, usually in the middle of a lot of blue, which showed the position of the ship she was working on.

"She's off the coast of South America," Ted Mole might say. Or, "I think she's just about to reach Australia."

"I wish she didn't have to be away so much," said Freddie rather sadly. "I can't wait for her to come home."

But he knew he would have to wait—and so did his father. Ted Mole put his arm about his son. "I know what you mean, Freddie," he said. "It's very hard, but I'm afraid we have no choice. I can't earn enough money doing my job, and so Ma has to take the only job she can find—which is on those ships. I'm sorry about that, but that's the way things are."

He was right, of course. Although Ted Mole worked very hard in his job as a wash-

ing machine repairman, he did not earn a great deal of money. This was because there were times when he did not have enough work, but it was also because his customers were often short of money and could not pay very much for their washing machines to be repaired.

Mrs. Mole sent back money from the ports her ships called in at, but most of what she sent went toward food. The twins were hearty eaters because they were growing so quickly, and Ted Mole found that the grocery bills grew larger day by day. Then there was the cost of clothes for the family. Freddie did not have many new clothes, but the twins grew out of things so quickly that it seemed that Ted had to buy new clothes for them almost every month.

"I don't want them to stay the same size forever," he complained. "But I do wish they wouldn't grow quite so fast."

It would have been easier for Ted Mole if he had only had to look after his own small family, but he had other people who relied on him, too. His brother, Stanley Mole, had hurt

his leg badly in an accident, and was unable to work as a result. He had six children to support, so Ted Mole had to give him money to make sure nobody went hungry in that family. As a result, at the end of the month there was hardly ever any money left—just a couple of coins, and that would never buy very much: a few potatoes, perhaps, or half a loaf of bread.

"I wish we weren't quite so poor," said Freddie to his father. "I wish I could earn some money to help you."

Ted Mole shook his head. "That's kind of you," he said. "But you have to go to school and learn. That way you'll be able to get a good job one day. Think how you can help us all then."

Freddie knew that his father was right,

but he still wished he could do something. He dreamed of ways of making some money. Perhaps he would invent something that everybody needed. Perhaps he would stumble across a nugget of gold in the stream that ran near his house. He had read about a man who had found a diamond when he was digging in the sand. At first he thought it was just any old rock, but when he washed it and it began to sparkle he knew that it was something very valuable. The man who found that diamond had been very poor—but no longer. That showed it could happen.

But we know, don't we, that things like that happen to other people. They never happen to us.

"Has anybody ever found a diamond near where we live?" asked Freddie.

His father shook his head. "No," he said. "Never."

"Or dug up any gold?"

Again Ted Mole shook his head. "Not here," he said. "There are places where you can find gold, but they're far away, I think. Australia, maybe."

Ted Mole looked at his son. He knew how much Freddie wanted to help, but there was no point in having false hopes. Yet there was no reason, he thought, why you should not have your dreams.

"Life can be very hard, my dear," he said to Freddie one evening as he tucked him into bed. "But let me tell you something."

Freddie waited for his father to continue.

"Sometimes," Ted Mole went on, "sometimes, good things happen when you least expect them. So the important thing is this: never give up hope."

"I won't," said Freddie as he closed his eyes for sleep. "I promise I won't."

"Good," said his father. "Because you never know what's going to happen, do you?"

★ ★ ★

Because Freddie was so popular at school, his friends often asked him to go on outings with them. So Freddie was invited to go bowling and swimming. He was invited to go to the cinema, where his friends would buy him large tubs of popcorn. He was given tickets to football matches where his friends' fathers had good seats near the front. He enjoyed all this, of course, but at the same time he felt awkward about not being able to repay such acts of kindness.

"Don't worry," said his friends. "You don't have to pay us back. It doesn't matter."

But it did matter to Freddie. "One day I'll do something for them," he said to himself. "I don't know when it will be, or how it will come about, but I'll do it."

It was one of these friends, Luke, who said to Freddie one day, "Would you like to go to the circus? You know that circus on the other side of town? Well, my dad has bought tickets. There'll be one for you, if you'd like it."

Freddie did not need any time to think about his answer. "Of course I would!" he exclaimed. "I'd like that very much."

Luke asked him whether he had ever been to a circus.

"No," said Freddie. "I've read about them, but I've never actually been to one."

"They're very exciting," said Luke. "We went last year. They had people who swung on trapezes, and a strong man who could tear telephone directories in half. And clowns, of course."

Freddie's eyes widened in delight. It all sounded like just the sort of thing he would like to see.

"And lions," continued Luke.

Freddie's eyes opened even wider. "In the tent?" he asked.

"Yes," said Luke. "They had a large cage, you see, that they set up in the ring. Then the lions came in and roared and sat on stools and roared again. It was really scary."

"I've heard of all that," said Freddie. "But I never thought I'd see it."

"Well, you will," said Luke. "You'll see it all tomorrow—and I know you'll like it."

Now, let's talk about lions in circuses. If you go to a circus today, you will *not* see lions—so don't be disappointed when there's not a single lion about. But remember, this story took place when circuses still had lions. That was not all that long ago, of course.

What happened to the lions you used to see in circuses? Well, many people thought it was rather unkind to keep lions in a circus, and I think these days most people agree with them. Lions are wild creatures, and it cannot be much fun being made to jump up on stools in a cage while hundreds of people look at you and shout and squeal. So circuses stopped having lions and became all about people who can do extraordinary things on a trapeze or be fired, as a human cannon-ball, out of great guns. That is certainly bet-ter for the lions; they were all sent off to nicer places—to zoos, where they have more room to live their lives without performing, or, in some cases, to game parks, which are almost as good as being back in the wild.

But in those days, there were still lions in the circus, and that night Freddie dreamed about them. He was not sure how many there were, or what they were doing, but there were lions in his dreams—great fierce crea-tures with dark manes and yellow eyes that looked right through him. It was not exactly a nightmare, but he was still glad when he woke up and realized that the lions had been dream lions all along.

The next day was exciting for more than one reason. Not only was there the trip to the circus, but it was also the last day of school before summer. That was always a wonderful day, as everybody looked forward to the long stretches of doing exactly what you wanted to do, rather than having to go off to school every morning. If you combine that feeling with the sense of excitement that goes with an imminent outing to the circus, you can imagine how Freddie felt.

The circus took place under a very large tent topped with a line of brightly colored flags. All around it were vans and trailers, some of them small, some of them big. This was where the circus supplies were kept—things the performers needed for their acts, food for the animals—and of course there were also the caravans in which the circus people lived. It was like a whole extra town—although a not very large one—attached to the edge of the real town.

Luke's parents led the way to the circus entrance. There they handed in their tickets at a booth before being directed into the tent itself. That was a very exciting moment, as it was just like entering a great cave filled with lights, music, and the smell of canvas. In the center was a ring, on the floor of which sawdust had been sprinkled. Around the ring, climbing up the sides of the tent, was row upon row of wooden seats.

The tent soon filled with people, and before long every seat was taken. Luke and Freddie had a very good view, as they were right down in the first row, one of the very

best places to be. They sat there, on the edge of their seats with excitement, while the band played and the lights began to dim.

Now it was dark except for a beam of light playing on the ring of sawdust. At this point the band stopped, all but the drums, which grew louder and louder. Then, in a flash of light, a man in a red tailcoat and black top hat leapt into the ring and made a low bow.

"The ringmaster," whispered Luke's father. "He's the most important man in the whole circus."

"Ladies and gentlemen!" shouted the ringmaster. "Boys and girls! The circus will now begin!"

With that, he gave another bow. Then the lights came up again, and Freddie watched in fascination as a man and a woman in gold outfits skipped into the ring, waved to the audience, and began climbing two ladders that soared up to the very top of the tent, high above the heads of the audience.

"Please be very quiet!" shouted the ringmaster. "For what you are about to see is a terribly, terribly dangerous act and any slip, even the smallest slip—could lead to . . ." He paused, and the tent became completely silent. ". . . could lead to DISASTER!"

Somebody in the audience squealed in fear but was drowned out by the roll of the drums as the two performers reached a platform at the top of the tent. There were two swings up there—two trapezes— and the performers now took hold of these and swung out over the emptiness below.

Freddie held his breath. The ringmaster had been right: this was terribly dangerous.

But then Freddie saw the net. It was right down near the ground, but it would have broken their fall if they had slipped and tumbled. It was still a very long way down, he thought, and he did not think he would care to fall that far.

There were many other acts, and every

one of them was thrilling. Just as Luke had predicted, there were lions. That, for Freddie, was the highlight of the evening. He had never seen a real lion before, and now there were four of them, all snarling and showing their fangs to the lion tamer and the audience. Each time they roared, a shiver ran through the crowd.

"You'd never get me in there," whispered Luke, pointing to the cage in which the lion act took place.

Freddie thought for a moment. Would he ever be brave enough to get that close to a group of four large lions—or even to *one* lion? He thought not, but then, he would never have the chance.

Or so he thought. But sometimes the things we think are wrong. Sometimes we can be very wrong about what lies ahead of us, and things that you imagine are unlikely—or even quite impossible—come about. And for Freddie, they did. This is what happened.

During the school holidays, Freddie would sometimes help his father fix washing machines. While the twins went off to their grandmother's house, Freddie would go with his father in the van. They would work all morning, Freddie helping him tighten nuts and bolts and passing him tools as he needed them. Then they would eat their sandwiches together at lunchtime, sitting in the van. Freddie felt very important doing this—it was just as if he had a real job; although, of course, his father did not pay him.

On the day after he had visited the circus, Freddie went with his father on his rounds. It was a busy day, as a lot of washing machines had broken down, and there was a great deal of work to do. But while they ate their lunch, Freddie told Ted Mole all about the night at the circus and about how much he and Luke had enjoyed it.

"There were some very funny clowns," he said. "They sprayed foam over one another. And there were some performing dogs and people who swung on a high trapeze."

"It sounds just like the circuses I used to go to when I was a boy," said Ted Mole. "I shall never forget them."

"And there were lions," Freddie continued. "There were four large lions that roared and snarled like this. . . ." He tried to imitate the lions, but of course, the sound he made was nowhere near as frightening as the sound of the real lions.

"Oh yes," said Ted Mole. "Never liked lions much myself, you know. Nasty creatures. Bite you if they get half the chance." He looked at his watch. "Lunchtime's up, Freddie. Time to get back to work."

They worked hard until three o'clock, when they went back to Ted Mole's workshop to tidy up and put the tools away. It was while they were doing this that the telephone rang. "Looks like we might be working late, Freddie," his father said as he put the phone to his ear. "Hello? Ted Mole, washing machine repairs . . ."

Freddie did not hear the other side of the conversation. All he heard was his father agreeing to come as soon as possible. Then Ted Mole put the phone down and turned to his son.

"You'll never guess," he said. "You'll never guess who that was. Any idea?"

Freddie shook his head.

"The ringmaster of that circus you went to," said Ted with a smile. "They have a washing machine in one of the vans. They use it for the performers' outfits, apparently."

"It's broken?"

Ted Mole nodded. "They're expecting us in about half an hour—so we'll just get the tools together again and be on our way."

As they prepared to set off, Freddie felt excitement grow within him. He had caught only the slightest glimpse of what went on behind the scenes at the circus. Now he would have a chance to see much more. And he would also meet the ringmaster, who might be able to introduce him to the clowns.

Waiting for something you really want to happen can make time drag. It did drag that afternoon—in fact, thought Freddie, it was the longest half hour he could remember. Eventually, though, they finished, and were off on their way to the field at the edge of town, where the circus was waiting for them.

The ringmaster met them at the entrance. He was not wearing his tail coat and top hat yet, but was dressed in ordinary clothes. He shook hands with Ted Mole and then with Freddie.

"It's good of you to come so quickly," he said. "We need that machine for our costumes. Working in a circus can be a dirty business, and we all need to look smart. So if our washing machine stops working, it's a big problem."

He led them to a large van with double doors that had been left open. Inside the van were several baskets of unwashed laundry standing outside one of the largest washing machines Freddie and his father had ever seen.

Ted gave a whistle. "That's a bit of a monster," he said. "I've never tackled anything like that."

"I'm sure you'll have no difficulty," said the ringmaster. "And while you're looking at it, I'll go off and get you each a mug of tea."

Circus tea! thought Freddie, and smiled with pleasure.

Ted Mole rolled his sleeves up and set to work on the unusual washing machine.

"Can you see what's wrong?" asked Freddie as he crouched beside his father.

From under the machine, Ted Mole mumbled his answer. "The thing that goes round and round is caught against the thing that goes up and down," he said. "And the two things that go in and out are going sideways instead. It won't take long to sort this out."

He asked Freddie to pass him a tool, and then another one. There followed a certain amount of banging and clattering before at last Ted reappeared from under the machine, wiped his face with a cloth, and pronounced the machine fixed.

The ringmaster had only just returned with two mugs of tea and was astonished that the machine had been repaired so quickly.

"Come to my office," he said. "You can drink your tea there and I'll pay you for the repair."

They followed him to a van that was parked near the entrance. This had OFFICE painted on it in large red letters. Inside were

a desk, a cupboard, and a large safe for the money from the tickets. Ted Mole told the ringmaster what his charge was and was paid immediately. Then they sat down in two chairs on the other side of the ringmaster's desk while he told them all about the circus.

"We're doing very well," he said. "We're a bit short of people, though. One of the ladies who helps about the place has gone off to have a baby, and our assistant—we have one who helps during the school holidays—has decided that he doesn't want to work anymore. All he wants to do is sit around, I believe. So that's not much good."

"Useless boy," said Ted Mole.

"Yes," said the ringmaster. "Hopeless. Why sit around when *not* sitting around is so much more exciting?"

Freddie said nothing at first, but he glanced at his father. Then he plucked up all his courage to speak. "Couldn't you get somebody else?" he asked.

The ringmaster shrugged. "I put up a notice," he replied. "It said HARDWORKING YOUNGSTER WANTED—GOOD WAGES. But do you know what? Not a single person answered— not one!"

"All too busy sitting around," said Ted Mole. "Lazy bunch."

Freddie looked at his father again. Then he shifted his gaze to the ringmaster. "Some people like working," he said in a small voice.

The ringmaster stared at him. "No doubt some do," he said. "But where are they? I ask myself."

Freddie felt his heart thumping within his chest. "There's one sitting right in front of you," he said.

Both men were now staring at Freddie.

"You mean . . . ?" began the ringmaster. "That is, you're talking about *yourself*?"

"My boy is a very hard worker," said Ted Mole. "He helps me on his holidays. He passes me my tools, and he's pretty good at tightening nuts and bolts, I can tell you."

"And I clean up afterwards," added Freddie. "If there's any oil on the ground, I mop it up. Same with water."

Ted Mole nodded. "He's a very clean boy," he said. "One of the cleanest boys in the country, I'm told. And I don't just say that because he's my son. Everybody says so."

There was a silence. Freddie looked down

at the ground. He was a modest boy and would never sing his own praises, but he was glad that his father had done so for him. And now, when he raised his eyes a little, he saw the ringmaster looking at him intently.

The ringmaster cleared his throat. "Would you be interested in the job?" he asked. "The pay's good, and you're obviously a very hardworking boy. You'd get a free breakfast, lunch, and dinner—eating with the performers—and one of the circus families will let you have a bunk in their caravan. You can have one day off a week to go home to see your family. How about it?"

Freddie held his breath. He looked at his father. *Please say yes*, he thought. *Please, please, please!*

Ted Mole hesitated for a few moments. "I don't know," he said. "I'm not sure that . . ." He stopped. He had seen the look on his son's face, and he knew what it meant.

"All right," he said. "You can work here, Freddie. Just for the holidays, mind."

Freddie jumped to his feet and threw his arms around his father. "Thank you," he whispered.

The ringmaster smiled. "That's what I like to see," he said. "A boy who knows how to work but who also knows how to say thank you. When can you start?"

"Tomorrow?" said Freddie.

"Then tomorrow it is," said the ringmaster. "First thing in the morning. We'll be expecting you."

★　★　★

Ted Mole dropped Freddie off at the circus bright and early the next morning.

"You've remembered your toothbrush?" he asked.

Freddie pointed to his bag. "It's in there," he said.

"And your clean sock?" Being poor, Freddie only had one spare sock, which he would change with one of his other socks each day. That way he never had to wear any sock for more than two days in a row.

Again Freddie gestured to his bag.

Ted Mole looked at his son. "Be careful," he said. "And work hard."

Freddie felt a lump in his throat. He had never been away from home before, and for a moment he wondered whether he was doing the right thing. His father seemed to sense this, as the next thing he said was that it was not too late for Freddie to change his mind.

And Freddie almost did—but not quite, and so he stepped back and waved to his father, who waved back before he drove off. Freddie watched his father's van disappear down the road before he turned round and made his way to the office. There he saw the ringmaster standing on the steps, waiting for him.

"Right," said the ringmaster. "You can start straightaway, Freddie. Your first job is to sweep up the mess that people left in the tent at last night's show. Messy bunch—they toss their bits of paper and peanut shells and heaven knows what down between the seats. It's a terrible job clearing it up—your job, in fact."

Freddie took the broom and the sack into which he was to put all the rubbish. Then he went into the tent and climbed between the seats to get to the space underneath. Just as the ringmaster had said, there was a lot of litter. There were ice cream wrappers and empty popcorn containers; there were tickets and scraps of paper; there were half-eaten hamburgers and hot dogs; there was even a hat and a single glove.

Freddie picked everything up. The hat and the glove he kept separately, as he thought he would hand them over to the ringmaster in case anybody claimed them. The rest he stuffed into the sack, which was soon almost completely full. But he picked up every last scrap of litter, and when the ringmaster came along to inspect his work, he was clearly pleased.

"Well done, Freddie!" he exclaimed. "The

last boy was very idle when it came to picking up litter. He left almost as much as he picked up. Well done!"

Because he had done his first chore so well, the ringmaster said Freddie could go off and have breakfast in the dinner tent, where all the circus people ate. Afterwards, he was to report to the cook to help with the washing up. And after that, he could help feed some of the animals.

Breakfast was in full swing when Freddie entered the dinner tent, but a woman pointed to a spare seat next to her and gestured for him to sit down.

"You're new, aren't you?" she said as he took the seat.

"Yes," said Freddie, looking about shyly. "I'm the new boy."

"Well, I'm Lisa," said the woman. "And this is Godfrey." She pointed to the man sitting on the other side of her. He smiled and stretched out a hand for Freddie to shake.

"We're the trapeze artists," said Lisa.

"I saw you when I came to the show," said Freddie. "You were terrific."

"Bless you!" said Lisa. "What a nice thing to say. Did you hear that, Godfrey? The new boy said we were terrific."

"Very civil of you," said Godfrey, nodding towards Freddie. "The last boy didn't have your manners."

"He certainly did not," agreed Lisa. "Nor the one before him, and the one before that one. Very rude and lazy boys they were."

A man in a cook's outfit emerged from the

back of the tent, carrying a plate. He put this down in front of Freddie.

"The boss said you did a very good job clearing up," he said cheerfully. "He says you deserve a good breakfast."

Freddie looked down at his plate. He was very hungry—not only because he had been working so hard, but also because money was short at home and they had not been able to buy much food over the last week. Now before him was a plate of sausages, two fried eggs, several rashers of bacon, a tomato, and a large and delicious-looking mushroom.

"Tuck in," said the cook. "And after you've finished, you're to come to the kitchen and help with the washing up."

Freddie savored every morsel of the delicious breakfast. It was just the right amount, and when he was finished, his stomach felt pleasantly full. It was a long time since he had felt full like that, and he thought it a very good feeling indeed.

But he was not going to sit around feeling full, and straightaway he left the table and made his way into the kitchen, where the cook was waiting for him. Also waiting was a high pile of dirty plates, saucepans, and cups.

Once the cook had shown him what to do,

Freddie set to work. It was not an easy task—dipping each plate into hot soapy water, giving it a good scrub with a brush, and then drying it and stacking it away. But he worked quickly, and within half an hour every plate was gleaming on the rack, ready for the next meal. The cook was pleased, and gave Freddie a pat on the back.

"Much better than the last boy," he said. "The plates were even dirtier when he finished washing them than when he started. Sloppy, greasy boy, that one!"

Freddie was pleased with the praise. And he was pleased, too, when the cook gave him an apple from the stores as a reward for his good work.

* * *

By the time lunchtime came around, Freddie had performed most of his day's work.

"You're very quick," said the ringmaster. "You can take the afternoons off if you carry on working at this pace. Then you can be on duty again for the evening show."

"But what can I do in the afternoon?" Freddie asked.

The ringmaster looked surprised. "Why, that's when everybody practices," he said.

"Practices?" asked Freddie.

"Practices their acts," said the ringmaster. "A good performer practices every day without fail. How else do you think they manage to make hard things look easy? Practice, my boy, practice!"

"But I . . . ," began Freddie.

"Of course you'll have to practice," said the ringmaster. "You're the understudy. Didn't I tell you that?"

Freddie looked confused. He was not sure what an *understudy* was. And if he did not know what it was, then how could he *be* one?

"Ah," said the ringmaster. "I see the

problem. You don't know what an understudy is, do you?"

Freddie shook his head.

"Well," began the ringmaster, "'understudy' is a word we use in the circus—but it's also a word they use in the theater, or in any sort of show. Are you with me so far?"

Freddie nodded hesitantly.

"So the understudy," continued the ringmaster, "is the person who takes over in place of a performer who's ill, for example, or who takes a holiday. An understudy is a sort of substitute. Do you follow me now?"

Freddie stared at the ringmaster in disbelief. He had never imagined that he would have to appear in the show. The idea was as frightening as it was exciting.

The ringmaster thought for a moment

before he spoke. Then he said, "So this afternoon Lisa and Godfrey will show you the ropes—if I may use that expression." He laughed at his joke, but Freddie did not.

"Y-you mean the trapeze?" stuttered Freddie.

"Yes," said the ringmaster. "I expect you'll love it. Not that the last boy did. He kept losing his grip and falling. I can't understand why. No head for heights, perhaps. Dizzy boy!"

Freddie swallowed hard. *I must be brave,* he thought.

★ ★ ★

His heart beating hard within him, Freddie poked his head round the flap of canvas at the main entrance to the big tent. It was dark inside, apart from a pool of light around the ring.

"Freddie!" called a voice from the darkness. He recognized it as Lisa's.

And then another voice came from somewhere above. "Lisa will help you up." That was Godfrey.

Freddie advanced slowly towards the ring. As he did so, Lisa emerged from the shadows. She was wearing the sparkling costume he had seen at the show.

"Here," she said, handing Freddie an outfit made of the same spangled material. "This should fit you. You can change in the ticket booth."

Freddie did as he was told, donning the unfamiliar costume. It felt very strange to be wearing something like that when he had no idea at all how to use a trapeze. But, once changed, he went back to the ring and stood, shivering ever so slightly, at Lisa's side.

"Don't be nervous," she said. "It looks very dangerous, but it's really completely safe. The net, you see, will catch you if you fall. You'll just bounce."

Freddie cast his eyes upwards. "Are you sure?"

Lisa laughed. "Of course I'm sure." She took him by the hand and led him to a rope ladder. "Look, let me show you. We'll climb to that platform up there—where the trapeze is—and then I'll let go and fall. You'll see how the safety net works. Then you can do the same."

Freddie gasped. "Fall?" he asked.

"Yes," she said. "It's very simple. Just let go of the trapeze and see what happens. You'll fall, of course, but you'll land in the net and bounce up. It's great fun, you know."

For a few moments Freddie toyed with the idea of running away. If he turned on his heels and ran, then he could just carry on running until he came to the main road. He could catch a bus there and be home in no time at all. But if he did that, then it would be the end of his job at the circus, and he was so looking forward to his wages.

Then he thought of his mother, working so hard for such long hours on those distant ships. She had to do things she did not want to do—she would far rather be at home, he thought—and yet she never complained. If she could do that for the good of the family, then the least he could do was to try to earn a bit of money. And if that meant he had to swing on a trapeze, then that was what he would do.

He turned to Lisa. "I'm ready," he said.

She smiled encouragingly. "Good," she said. "Then let's start climbing."

It did not take long to reach the platform up at the top. Godfrey was waiting for them there, holding on to a trapeze with one hand while he used the other to help them onto the platform.

"Freddie is going to have a bit of practice with the net," said Lisa. "I'll go first."

"Righty-ho," said Godfrey, passing the trapeze to her. "Here you are."

Lisa placed both her hands on the trapeze. "I'm just going to swing a few times," she explained to Freddie. "Then I'll let go and fall. Watch me hit the net down below and bounce back. It's quite simple, you know—nothing to it!"

Turning around, she bent her knees and launched herself off the edge of the platform.

"There she goes," said Godfrey. "Swinging nicely, just like . . ." He suddenly stopped, and Freddie knew immediately that something was wrong.

"Oh no," gasped Godfrey. "I forgot to put the net up!"

Horrified, Freddie looked out over the emptiness. Lisa was swinging energetically on the trapeze, bending her legs to give her more movement.

"Lisa!" shouted Godfrey. "Don't let go! Don't let go!"

From the other side of the tent, there came a faint voice in reply. "What was that you said?"

Godfrey cupped his hands to make his voice louder. "I said DON'T LET GO!"

"Don't get low?" came the faint—and puzzled—reply.

"No, DON'T LET GO!"

Godfrey now turned to Freddie. "Freddie," he said. "How quickly can you slide down a rope?"

Freddie realized that this was a real emergency. "Very quickly," he said. He hoped this was true.

"Right," said Godfrey. "I'm going to stay up here and try to attract Lisa's attention. You slide down this rope as quickly as you can. At the bottom you'll see a red box with a button. That controls the machine that will wind the safety net into position. Press it the moment you get down. Understand?"

Freddie nodded. Without any hesitation he seized the rope that Godfrey passed him, wrapped his legs round it, and jumped.

Down he slid, much faster than he had imagined possible, but slowly enough to land softly when he reached the bottom. Once there, he picked himself up and raced across to the red control box. The button was there—exactly where Godfrey had said it would be—and when he pressed it he heard the welcome sound of machinery unwinding the safety net.

Up above, Godfrey had managed to get his warning to Lisa, but now that the net was in place, she was free to let go. And she did, tumbling like an angel falling out of the sky.

Freddie watched from below. He held his breath as Lisa came down, and then let it out in a relieved rush when he saw how the net broke her fall. And then he watched in astonishment as he saw her bounce up, turn an elegant somersault in the air, and then fall back into the net. It all looked so easy and so comfortable. It looked like fun, too.

"Your turn, Freddie," called Lisa as she lowered herself from the edge of the safety net.

Freddie was still standing on the ground, and he looked up at the platform high above him. It seemed an impossible distance to fall and not get hurt, but he had seen it done now, and he was not as frightened as he had been earlier.

"Yes," he said. "I'm coming."

It was such fun that he did it three times, letting go, being bounced up by the net, and then climbing back up the rope ladder to

let go once again. At the end of net practice, Godfrey and Lisa gave him several les-
sons in swinging on the trapeze. After that
they showed him how Godfrey could hook
his knees over the trapeze and then, while
hanging upside down, hold on to Freddie. He
would swing across like that and pass Freddie to Lisa, who was swinging towards him

on another trapeze. Freddie did not have to do anything in that trick, but had to allow himself to be grasped by the trapeze artists as one might grasp a parcel.

"See how simple it is?" said Godfrey. "In fact, I think you're ready to join us in our act tonight."

Freddie's jaw dropped. "In the show? Tonight?"

"I don't see why not," said Godfrey. And then to Lisa he said, "Do you agree, Lisa?"

Lisa nodded. "Freddie's a star," she said. "He's got it written all over him." She paused before adding, "Welcome to the show, Freddie."

* ★ ★ ★

Have you ever tried not to feel nervous? It's very difficult, isn't it? You tell yourself you're not afraid, but that just seems to make it worse. You say to yourself, *My hands aren't shaking,* but of course when you look at them they are. And that is exactly how Freddie felt as he waited outside the tent that night with Godfrey and Lisa. All three of them were wearing their sparkling trapeze-artist outfits, and all three were listening to the ringmaster's voice as he addressed the crowd inside.

"And now, ladies and gentlemen," he announced in echoing tones. "Now we have the act you have all been waiting for."

There was a murmur of excitement from the crowd.

"Now, ladies and gentlemen, fresh from their tour of the capitals of the world, fresh from their triumph at the International Circus Olympics—we are proud to present . . ." There was a roll of drums from the band—a low rumble that grew louder and louder until it ended in a clash of cymbals. "Ladies and gentlemen: the Flying Trio—the beautiful and lithe Lisa, star of the high trapeze; the great and fearless Godfrey, superman of the sky-high swings; and introducing the fearless and fantastic Freddie, junior champion of the tent-top!"

The band struck up raucously. *Pom, pom, pom de pom* . . . "That's the signal," said Godfrey, digging Freddie gently in the ribs. "That's our cue."

Freddie took a deep breath and followed Godfrey and Lisa as they ran into the tent. As he entered, his ears rang with the applause of the audience. "Look!" people shouted. "There they are!" yelled others.

The three of them took a deep bow and then began to climb up the rope ladder. Godfrey led the way, with Lisa behind him and Freddie bringing up the rear. As they made their way skywards, the crowd became hushed with anticipation, although there were a few oohs and aahs as people craned their necks to follow them.

When they reached the platform, Freddie

had to force him-
self to look down.
He was aware of the
faces of the crowd
far below him, and
he thought he could
make out the figure of
the ringmaster standing
at the edge of the ring,
peering upwards.

"Right," said Godfrey
as he moved one of the
two trapezes into posi-
tion. "I'm going to start
off swinging. You stand at
the edge, Freddie, and hold
out your arms.

"When I reach you, I'll grab you by your wrists and swing back with you. Then Lisa will swing out and I'll pass you over to her. She'll take your ankles and swing backwards and forwards five or six times, then swing back to the platform. Understood?"

He did not give Freddie any time to speak, but launched himself into the void. Lisa then moved Freddie to the edge of the platform and held on to him as Godfrey swung back in their direction.

Freddie stood quite still, trying not to look down. He saw Godfrey approaching him, hanging on the trapeze by his knees. Then everything happened rather quickly. He felt his wrists being seized in a firm grip, and he felt Lisa push him forwards. And suddenly he was in flight, gripped by

Godfrey, his feet pointed downwards, his stomach churning as they made an arc through the air.

They swung several times, and with each crossing there came gasps of wonder and admiration from the audience below. Freddie had calmed down by now, and felt rather proud of what he was doing. He was even enjoying himself, until he happened to look down and saw something that turned his heart cold with fear.

"The net!" he gasped. "You've forgotten the safety net again!"

Godfrey glanced down. "Oh?" he said. "Oh, how foolish of me. Well, don't worry, Freddie. We won't drop you."

"I want to get down," Freddie wailed.

"Oh, come on, Freddie," said Godfrey

cheerfully. "Everything's going to be fine. Look, Lisa's ready to take you now."

Freddie gave a moan as he was swung back to the platform and another moan as Lisa grabbed him and swung out on her trapeze. He was upside-down now, held by his ankles, and he noticed that the ringmaster was doing something down below. It was hard to make out exactly what that was, as he was swinging backwards and forwards so much, but then he realized what it was— the ringmaster was pressing the button on the safety net controls. And yes, there was the net moving into position.

It was just as well. Just as the net moved into position, Lisa said, "I'm going to have to sneeze." And then, as she sneezed, her grip slackened, and Freddie felt himself hanging by only one ankle, and then by none, and then he was falling through the air, head over heels, down towards the ground.

He felt the safety net yield beneath him. He felt himself bouncing up. He felt himself descending into the net again and bouncing once more. He heard the crowd clap and cheer.

He rose to his feet. A spotlight was shining on him and he knew what he had to do. He made a deep bow, and a roar of applause arose from the crowd. They thought that this was all planned—that the fall through the air was really a dive. They thought him very brave.

Freddie became aware that the ringmaster was standing next to him. He bowed to the crowd as well, and they cheered him, just as they had cheered Freddie.

"Well done, Freddie!" said the ringmaster from the side of his mouth. "Excellent boy! Oh, and by the way, I want you to help with the lions at tomorrow night's show—the lion tamer's assistant has gone off to Peru, of all places. So inconsiderate of him! But I told

Harry—he's the lion tamer—that you'd be happy to help."

Freddie froze. "Me?" he whispered. "Me?"

The ringmaster gave another bow to the crowd. He was smiling broadly, his white teeth flashing in the bright light of the ring.

"Yes, Freddie, you. You'll be fine, believe me. Nothing to worry about—nothing at all!"

★   ★   ★

Freddie did not enjoy his breakfast the next morning. Although the cook had made him a plate of his favorite—bacon and eggs— with an extra helping of mushrooms for good measure, he did not feel like eating. And how could he think of anything other than the dreadful ordeal that lay ahead of him?

"Not hungry this morning?" asked Lisa, who was sitting on the other side of the table.

Freddie shook his head. Lisa looked at him kindly. "Not feeling well?"

Freddie stared down at his plate of untouched breakfast. "No, it's not that at all. It's the lions."

Lisa frowned. "The lions? What about the lions?"

Freddie decided to tell her. "The ringmaster told me that I have to help Harry today. He says that Harry's assistant has gone off to Peru and so I have to take his place. And . . . and . . ." His voice faltered. Then he finished. "And I'm so scared."

For a moment Lisa said nothing. Then her face broke into a smile. "Oh, my goodness, you don't need to be scared of lions . . . or at least, not of *those* lions."

"But I saw them," protested Freddie.

"They are very large and they have great big teeth. And they roar in a very frightening way. . . ."

Lisa help up a hand to stop him. There was something amusing her.

"Listen, Freddie," she said. "It's perfectly normal to be frightened of lions. But those lions . . . Well, let me come with you. I'll have a word with Harry and he'll let me show you something."

Freddie was pleased that Lisa had agreed to come with him. He was still nervous, of course, but he liked Lisa, and having her with him cheered him up a bit.

As they left the table, Lisa pointed to Freddie's plate of untouched breakfast. "Those sausages," she said. "Bring them with you."

"But I'm not feeling hungry," said Freddie. "I don't want them."

"But the lions will," said Lisa. "Come on, bring them with you."

Freddie did as he was told, although he did not like the thought of feeding sausages to lions. How would a lion tell the difference between your fingers and a sausage? Would a lion even bother to tell the difference?

The lions were kept in a large metal cage right on the edge of the circus site. Harry, the lion tamer, was sitting in front of this cage, shaded from the sun by a large umbrella. He was filing his fingernails with a large nail file when they arrived, and he continued to do so as Lisa introduced Freddie.

"You're the new boy," he said, not looking up from his task of filing his nails. "I've heard all about you. They say you're much better than the last boy." He paused and looked up. "The lions didn't like him, you know. Oh no, they didn't take to that boy."

Freddie did not know what to say.

"You heard about my assistant?" Harry

continued. "He's gone off to Peru. Just like that. I've got half a mind to go myself, you know."

Lisa shook her head. "You can't go off to Peru, Harry," she said severely. "Who would look after your lions?"

Harry made a face. It was a very grumpy face. "Oh, they'd get somebody," he said. He glanced at Freddie. "Somebody young and keen."

Freddie looked down at the ground. He did *not* want to look after lions. He may have been young, but he was not in the slightest bit keen—not when it came to lions.

Lisa now suggested that Freddie should be introduced to the lions. "And don't worry," she whispered to him. "Nothing bad is going to happen."

"You go and show him, then," said Harry. "I don't care."

They went round to the side of the cage. Freddie looked warily through the bars and saw four large lions sleeping together in a sort of heap. As he and Lisa approached the door of the cage, one of the lions opened an eye and looked at them lazily.

"That one's Ripper," said Lisa. "And the one next to him is Growler. Then there's Roarer and Prowler."

The lions were stirring now. Seeing that they had visitors, they were stretching and scratching, shaking their magnificent manes.

"Give me the sausages," said Lisa.

Freddie passed her the sausages, which he had wrapped in a paper napkin. Lisa took them and reached for the handle to the cage door. "Are you coming with me?" she asked.

"Inside?" asked Freddie, his voice unsteady with fear.

Lisa did not seem the slightest bit scared. "Of course. Come on."

As they entered the cage, the lions took a few steps away from them. Freddie had not expected this, nor had he expected what happened next. Lisa held out the sausages, calling to the lions as she did so. "Come on, boys," she coaxed. "Nice sausages."

Very cautiously, the lions approached her, sniffed at the sausages, and then each took one in its mouth and sat down to chew it. Freddie watched in astonishment.

"Where are their teeth?" he asked.

Lisa smiled. "That's a good question,

Freddie," she said. "You see, these lions are
rather old. They used to have all their teeth,
but they lost most of them years ago. And
as for their claws, they still have them, but
they're dreadfully blunt."

"But I saw their teeth!" protested Freddie. "When I saw them in the show, they had
great sharp teeth."

Lisa shook her head. "False teeth," she said. "Made of plastic. Harry fits them in each lion just before the performance. They can't really bite anything with them. And when they don't have them in, they find it a bit difficult to eat anything that needs to be chewed. Even these sausages are a bit of an effort for them."

"But they were very fierce," went on Freddie. "I heard them roar."

"Oh, they roar, all right," said Lisa. "But they don't really mean it. They've been trained to act fierce in the circus ring, but actually they would never so much as say boo to a goose. They're very gentle lions, these ones—in spite of their names."

Freddie watched as Lisa bent down to pat Growler, just as one might pat a friendly cat.

The lion arched his back and began to purr.

"There," said Lisa. "You see how friendly he is, Freddie. Why don't you go and pat Prowler—we don't want him to feel left out."

Freddie approached Prowler gingerly. The lion watched him and then suddenly stepped forward, making Freddie give a start. But it was only to lick Freddie's hand, which was what Prowler now did.

"He likes you," said Lisa. "That's the biggest compliment a lion can pay, you know—to lick you like that."

Freddie smiled at the thought. He had decided that he liked the lions, and he was pleased to discover that they liked him, too. Over the next half hour they got to know one another even better. Lisa showed him the games the lions liked to play, including

fetch-the-ball, lion-tag, and hide-and-seek. Then they left them, as Freddie had to go off and help polish the spotlights.

"Good luck this evening," said Lisa.

"Thank you," replied Freddie. His fear had gone, and he was looking forward to the evening show, when he would enter the lion's cage with Harry and his new friends. He had never imagined—never in his wildest dreams—that he would be a lion tamer, but now that it was happening, he was rather proud of himself. *"Freddie Mole,"* he muttered under his breath. *"Freddie Mole, Lion Tamer."* Yes, it sounded rather good, he thought. Not that he was a boastful boy, but if something sounded rather good, one might as well mutter it.

★ ★ ★

The tent was full that night. Freddie watched as the crowds streamed in, and then took up a place near the entrance, ready to help Harry with the lions. Harry had lent him a uniform: a splendid pair of khaki jodhpurs—a special sort of riding trousers—a brown tunic top, and gleaming leather boots. "You look quite the lion tamer," said Lisa admiringly.

The circus started with the clowns. The crowd loved them, and roared with approval each time one clown threw a custard pie at another clown. Then there were the performing dogs and the dancing horses—both brought prolonged applause and cheers. After that, Lisa and Godfrey did their act, although they did not have Freddie to help them.

As the trapeze artists swung backwards and forwards at the top of the tent, the ringmaster made his way to Freddie's side.

"Where's Harry?" he asked. "Have you seen him this evening?"

Freddie shook his head. "He told me to meet him here ten minutes before we were due to go on. But he hasn't turned up yet."

The ringmaster glanced at his watch. "It's too bad," he complained. "Harry promised me that he would never miss another performance. Now he appears to be doing exactly that."

"I'm sure he'll turn up," said Freddie.

"Well, I'm not so sure," snapped the ringmaster. "I suspect that he's gone off to Peru or somewhere like that. He's let us down before." He looked at his watch again. "He's got another four minutes—that's all."

Freddie felt a pang of disappointment. He had been looking forward to getting into the ring with lions, and he did not want the show to be cancelled. Without thinking too much about it, he made his offer.

"I'll do it," he said.

The ringmaster looked at him in astonishment. "By yourself?" he asked.

Freddie swallowed hard. Was he brave enough? He thought of the lions—they *looked* fierce, but he understood they were really rather shy. And as for their teeth—he knew they were false and could not really bite. And he knew, too, that their claws were blunt. . . . He made up his mind. "Yes," he said. "I want to help."

The ringmaster was doubtful—but only for a moment. Then he smiled, thumped Freddie on the back in a friendly way, and said, "That's my boy! That's the true spirit of the circus! You're on, Freddie!"

The lions had already been moved into a small pen near the big tent. Together with the ringmaster, Freddie now went there while, inside the tent, their show cage was being assembled. The lions were eager to begin the show, as they always received

treats for performing. They were very obedient, sitting down without complaint and
opening their mouths widely for the fitting
of their false teeth. That took only a few moments, and then they impatiently, but very
politely, followed Freddie in a long line back
to the circus tent itself.

Once Lisa and Godfrey finished their
act and had taken their final bow, the ringmaster entered the tent. Waving his top hat
in the air to show that he was about to make
an announcement, he shouted: "And now,
ladies and gentlemen, the most thrilling part
of this evening's entertainment—the lions,
those four kings of the jungle, Ripper, Roarer,
Growler, and Prowler, with their trainer, the
world-famous, or soon to be world-famous,
Freddie Mole!"

Hearing this, Freddie blushed to the roots

of his hair. He was not world-famous, but then, everything the ringmaster said was a little bit made up, and perhaps that was just the way circuses worked. But there was no time to worry too much about that. Hearing the roars of the crowd inside, the lions themselves gave an answering roar, and in they all bounded, followed by Freddie.

Freddie really had very little to do. The lions knew their part exactly, and they immediately leapt up onto large metal stools, fixed the crowd with fierce glares, and growled in the most convincing way. As Freddie walked past him, Ripper let out a particularly vicious snarl and took a swipe at him. Many members of the crowd screamed when they saw this, and one girl actually fainted—for a few seconds—but was quickly revived by

ice cream. For his part, Freddie knew that Ripper was only acting—and this was confirmed by Ripper himself, who gave Freddie a friendly wink as he passed.

The lions went through their paces. They roared and growled and slunk their way round the ring, and even had a small lion-fight among themselves. Freddie, of course, could see that this fight was entirely friendly—the lion version of a playful pillow fight—but nobody in the audience was to know that.

When the lions had done their final tricks, they scampered back to their home cages, leaving Freddie in the ring to take the applause. And that applause was very loud. "Bravo!" some shouted, which means *Well done!* while others shouted, "Bravissimo!"

which means *Very, very well done!* Freddie bowed very politely to thank everybody for these compliments. Then he took a step back to bow again, and he noticed something that he had missed in his excitement. Sitting in the cheap seats at the back of the tent was his father, and . . . He stared into the crowd. Could it possibly be? Surely not.

But it was. There was his father, and there, at his side, was . . . his mother.

"Ma!" shouted Freddie, and waved.

Freddie's mother stood up in her seat and waved back. Then his father stood up and waved as well. All eyes in the crowd turned to stare at the two standing figures. People were a bit puzzled. Who were these people at the back who were standing up and waving?

"It's my father and mother!" shouted Freddie. "It's them!"

The crowd loved this, and people immediately began to clap for Freddie's parents. "I bet they're brave, too!" shouted a woman sitting nearby. Then a man at the front called out, "They should come and take a bow! After all, they must have brought their son up to be brave—they deserve the credit for that!"

This suggestion brought a chorus of approval. Although very modest people, Ted and Flora Mole were proud of their son, and this was his moment. So they made their way down the aisle between seats and entered the ring. Freddie rushed forward to meet them, flinging himself into his mother's arms. This was the signal for the crowd to cheer even more loudly than ever. "There's a boy who loves his mother!" shouted somebody, and another yelled, "He looks just like his dad—just as handsome!"

"You didn't tell me you had become a lion tamer, my darling," said Freddie's mother.

"I'm so proud of you—standing there like that with those fierce lions."

"To tell the truth, Ma," whispered Freddie, "they're not fierce at all. They just look it."

Ted Mole laughed. "Their teeth were frightening enough."

"False," Freddie muttered. "False teeth, Dad. Just like Granny's."

"Oh well," said Ted Mole. "We all enjoyed it very much. And I'm so proud of you, son. I'm so proud I could burst."

After the crowd had left the tent, Freddie and his parents made their way out as well, but were stopped at the entrance by the ringmaster.

"Where do you think you're going?" he asked as he stepped out in front of them.

Freddie was worried. He thought the ringmaster might perhaps feel that he was going to try to escape doing some chore, such as cleaning up after the crowd. He would not dream of doing that, of course, as he was a hardworking boy and would never shirk any task.

"I was just going to say goodbye to my parents," said Freddie. "I was going to come back and pick up the rubbish—I promise I was."

The ringmaster laughed. "Oh, I didn't think you were shirking, Freddie—anything but that. No, I just wanted to invite you and your parents"—and here he bowed politely to the Moles—"to join me in the office for a celebration. Champagne for your parents, Freddie, and a fizzy drink for you. Not quite as fizzy as champagne, perhaps, but fizzy nonetheless."

They accepted the invitation and accompanied the ringmaster to the van marked OFFICE. There they were invited to sit down while the ringmaster poured the champagne and the other fizzy drink. Then he raised his glass to propose a toast. "To our brave lion tamer," he said. "To Freddie Mole."

Freddie thanked everybody and then took a sip of his soft drink.

"I'm really glad you're back, Ma," he said to his mother.

"And I'm glad to be back," Mrs. Mole said. "I only arrived back yesterday—from Cape Horn. It was very rough out there, I'm afraid. We had very high seas."

"Well, you're back safely, Madam," said the ringmaster. "I always say that dry land is far drier than the sea, would you not agree?"

"I do," said Mrs. Mole. "There are very few people who would disagree with you about that."

"The sea is undoubtedly very wet," said Ted Mole. "And when it's rough, it's rather like a great washing machine, I've always thought."

"I see," said the ringmaster. "And by that I mean *I see* rather than *I sea*."

Freddie, being polite, laughed at this, and the ringmaster was very pleased. Now he turned to Freddie's father and asked him how his washing machine repair business was doing. Ted Mole told him that it scraped along but that it never did all that well. The ringmaster nodded and looked very thoughtful at this, and he frowned when Ted told him that there were times when it was difficult to get customers to pay their bills once he had fixed their washing machine.

"Very inconsiderate," he said, shaking his head. "A hardworking man such as yourself, sir, deserves better than that."

There was a silence, and then the ringmaster said, "I've had an idea."

Everybody looked at him, waiting for the idea to be revealed.

"It's a very good idea," the ringmaster went on to say. "If you will permit me to tell you about it, I shall do so."

"Of course," said Ted Mole.

"Well," said the ringmaster, "I must tell you what an excellent boy your Freddie is. He's hardworking, polite, and ten times better than the last boy we had. No, in fact, he's *twenty* times better."

"Well done, son," said Ted Mole. "Your ma and I are proud of you."

"So you should be," said the ringmaster. "And here's my idea: Many people who work in circuses, as you know, work there because their whole family does. So I wondered whether you would all like to join my circus. I have no son, and eventually, when I retire, it will be necessary for the circus to be run by somebody else. I can think of no person more suited for that task—not just yet, of course, but at some date in the future—than young Freddie here. I really cannot think of anybody better."

Freddie caught his breath. Had he heard that correctly? Sometimes you hear nice things because you *want* to hear them and your mind invents them. Had the ringmaster really said all that?

The ringmaster now turned to Freddie's mother. "You, Mrs. Mole, would possibly like less . . . how shall I put it? . . . a less peripatetic job. Am I right?"

Freddie looked puzzled. *Peripatetic?* It sounded such a nice word, but what on earth did it mean?

Ted Mole saw his son's puzzled expression. " 'Peripatetic' means 'traveling around,' " he whispered. "It's a very good word."

Mrs. Mole told the ringmaster that he was indeed right. "When we were down at Cape Horn," she said, "and the ship was being tossed all over the place, I thought there must be easier ways of earning a living."

"I would give you a very fine caravan," said the ringmaster. "There would be plenty of room for you and your children. And

Freddie could go to school during the day and do the shows at night. I could put his acts in at the beginning of the program so he would be in bed by his proper bedtime."

"Very good," said Ted Mole. "A regular bedtime is very important—even if you are a lion tamer."

"Precisely," said the ringmaster.

Freddie looked at his father. It all sounded like such a wonderful chance, but he knew, as all children know, that there are times when grown-ups sometimes just do not see how wonderful a chance may be. "Please say yes," he whispered, so softly that almost nobody would be able to hear.

His father did hear, though, and he turned for a quick whispered discussion with his wife. Then he turned back to the ringmaster.

"We accept," he said. "As long as it's all right with Freddie."

"Of course it is," said Freddie quickly. "It's the best decision you've ever made, Dad."

His father shook his head. "No, the best decision I ever made, son," he said, "was to marry your ma here."

That is just the sort of thing wives like their husbands to say, and Mrs. Mole was very pleased. "And the best decision I ever made was to say yes when you asked me," she said.

"All very satisfactory," said the ringmaster. "So, when can you start?"

"Tomorrow," said Ted Mole. "I know somebody who wants to buy my washing machine repair business. I shall sell it to him first thing in the morning, and then we can pack up and come over."

"Even more satisfactory," said the ringmaster. "But I haven't mentioned your wages. This is what I shall pay you at the end of every month." He scribbled a figure on a piece of paper and handed it to Freddie's father. Ted Mole looked at it. His eyes opened wide.

"That's a lot of money," he said. "You're very generous."

"Hard work—and talent—deserve their reward," said the ringmaster.

The Mole family settled into their new life very happily. Ted Mole soon proved to be extremely useful about the place, fixing things and making sure everything worked smoothly. He even invented things that made circus life much easier, such as a way of putting the big tent up in half the normal time by using pulleys and winches. Mrs. Mole took over the performing dogs, as the dog lady had married a famous mountaineer and she wanted to go off and climb mountains in India with him. The dogs loved their new trainer, and together they invented all sorts of new tricks. Even the twins, although still tiny, found something to do. They became quite friendly with a tame wolf that the circus had, so the ringmaster set up a sideshow at the entrance to the tent. This was a cage which had written on it ROMULUS AND REMA, THE TWO WILD BABIES OF ROME. The show consisted of the twins sitting in the cage with the wolf, who nuzzled them and licked their faces in an affectionate way. The twins loved this, and every so often would howl like wolves, to the great amazement of the crowd that gathered around them.

Now that they had more money, the Mole family were able to buy smart new clothes. Freddie was bought five pairs of socks, so he could change them nearly every day. He also saved a lot, putting his money into a piggy bank that the ringmaster gave him for his birthday. Ted bought a new suit and a red and white car with large headlights. Mrs. Mole bought an armchair, a necklace of real pearls, and a whole shelf of books, as she loved reading stories about the sea. Everybody was much happier—not least because their work in the circus brought excitement and pleasure to so many people, and that was a very good thing. If you can make other people happier, then you become happier yourself. Everybody knows that.

And what happened to the lions? Well, here's an extraordinary story. The ringmaster had always wondered whether they would be better off in the wild, and one day he thought they should try to give them their freedom. So they sent the lions off to a game preserve in Africa, where they would be released to live an ordinary lion life.

The lions did not like it. It was not just their false teeth that were the problem; it was the whole business of being a lion in the wild. The wild, the lions thought, can sometimes be just a bit too wild. So they ran back to the game preserve office every time they were left out on the plains. Eventually the game reserve said that it was clear that the lions would be happier back at the circus, and so they were returned. They were delighted, jumping all over Freddie and licking his face like a pack of playful dogs.

And here's another extraordinary story. A few years ago—I think it was last year—I found myself passing through a town I had never visited before. I was on a train, and when the train drew out of the town, I suddenly noticed that we were going past a field in which a circus was camped. I looked out the window—it was raining, and the glass had little rivers of water coursing down it, so I could not see very well. But I did spot a large tent, and I did notice a flag on top of it, and I did see a sign that read FREDDIE MOLE'S CIRCUS.

I craned my neck to see more, but the train was gathering speed and the circus was disappearing behind us. After a few moments, the railway line curved away in the opposite direction and the circus was lost to view. But I saw it, and I was not mistaken about the sign and what it said. FREDDIE MOLE'S CIRCUS. Those three words, I thought, told a very big story.

About the Author

ALEXANDER McCALL SMITH is the author of the bestselling No. 1 Ladies' Detective Agency series. He has also written over thirty books for younger readers, including *School Ship Tobermory* and *The Sands of Shark Island*, as well as a series featuring the young Precious Ramotswe, one of the world's most famous fictional private detectives.

Visit him online at alexandermccallsmith.com and on Facebook, and follow him on Twitter at @McCallSmith.

FOR YOUNG READERS, INTRODUCING PRECIOUS AS A YOUNG GIRL

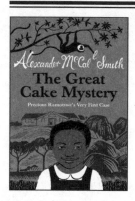

THE GREAT CAKE MYSTERY

In her first case as a young girl, Precious sets out to find the real thief of a piece of cake. Along the way she learns that your first guess isn't always right. She also learns how to be a detective.

Volume 1

THE MYSTERY OF MEERKAT HILL

Precious has a new mystery to solve! When her friend's family's most valuable cow vanishes, Precious must devise a plan to find the missing animal! But she needs the help of another to solve the case. Will she succeed and what obstacles will she face on her path?

Volume 2

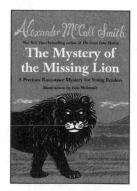

THE MYSTERY OF THE MISSING LION

Precious gets a very special treat: a trip to visit her aunty Bee at a safari camp. On her first day there, a new lion arrives. But this is no average lion: Teddy is an actor-lion who came with a film crew. When Teddy escapes, Precious and her resourceful new friend Khumo decide to use their detective skills to help track down the lion and find out where he has gone.

Volume 3

Illustration © Iain McIntosh